# The Adventures of OOK AND GLUK KUNG-FU CAVEMEN FROM The FUTURE

by George Beard and Harold Hutchins

For Connor Mancini

Scholastic Children's Books
An imprint of Scholastic Ltd
Euston House, 24 Eversholt Street
London, NW1 1DB, UK
Registered office: Westfield Road, Southam, Warwickshire, CV47 0RA
SCHOLASTIC and associated logos are trademarks and/or registered trademarks of Scholastic Inc.

First published in the US by Scholastic Inc, 2010
Published in hardback in the UK by Scholastic Ltd, 2010
This edition published in the UK by Scholastic Ltd, 2011

Text and illustration copyright © Dav Pilkey, 2010
Cover illustration copyright © Dav Pilkey, 2010

The right of Dav Pilkey to be identified as the author and
illustrator of this work has been asserted by him.

ISBN 978 1407 12401 8

A CIP catalogue record for this book is available from the British Library.

Printed and bound by CPI Group (UK) Ltd, Croydon, CR0 4YY
Papers used by Scholastic Children's Books are made from
wood grown in sustainable forests.

13

www.scholastic.co.uk/zone

# A SCIENTIFIC DISCLAIMER

By
Professor Gaylord M. Sneedly

The book you hold in your
hands contains many scientific errors and stuff.

For example, dinosaurs and cavemen did not live
at the same time. Dinosaurs lived more than 64
million years BEFORE cavemen.

And I should know! In 2003, I was the recipient
of The Most Brilliantest Science Guy of the
Whole Wide World Award.

So there!

# A Scientific Disclaimer Disclaimer

## By George and Harold

SCIENTISTS Think They Know everything!

BUT They dont!

They Just make guesses based on evidense Theyve already discovered.

I call my guesses "Theries" so They sound important!

← "Genius"

BUT Theres all Kinds of NEW evidense discovered every day!

So the "TRUTH" is always changing!

Forchenately, we have a Time machine.

Purple Potty Co.

4

We've Been To The Future and the Past!

So We discovered Lots of evidense That scientists dont Know About... YET!!!

For exampel: Some dinosaurs Did Live The Same Time as cavemen!

Hey

What Up?

But Scientists wont discover That until The year 2073!

So if your Looking for guesses, There are plenty of Science books To choose From.

The Origin OF Guesses

a Brief history of Guesses

Or you can Read The Worlds First Book Based on SCIENCE FACTS!!!

5

# CHAPTERS

# The Adventures of OOK AND GLUK

## KUNG-FU CAVEMEN FROM THE FUTURE

### CHAPTER 1
#### Meet OOK and GLUK

This is Ook Schadowski and Gluk Jones. Ook is the kid on the left with the missing tooth and the stringy haircut. Gluk is the kid on the right with the lepard spots and the afro.

remember that now!

Ook and Gluk lived way back in the year 500,001 B.C. in a villege called Caveland, Ohio.

welkum to Caveland

8

Another time when they were 7, they almost got ate up by Mog-Mog: The fearsest dinosaur in Caveland.

And once they even traveled to the future, learned Kung-Fu, and saved there whole villege from Evil Robots and time-traveling weirdos!

BUT BEFORE we can tell you that story, we have to tell you

THIS STORY

This is BiG cheif Goppernopper.

He was the Ruler of caveland and He hated Ook and Gluk.

Grrrr

Every time chief Goppernopper tried to be a big shot, Ook and Gluk always ruined it!

clank clank

Look at me! Me invented wheel!

SHOOM

Look at me! me created spear!

SNAP

BOOM

Look at me! me Discovered **FiRE!**

ZOOoooOM

Those two kids driving me CRAZY! Me need to sit on throne and relax!

What the?

OOK WUZ HERE GLUK too

GARDS!!

Here we are, cheif Grasshopper.

My names not Grass-Hopper, Its Goppernopper!!! Jeez, How many times me got to Tell you?

We sorry, Chief Gobstopper.

while you dummies were goofing off, my throne was defiled!

OOK WUZ HERE GLUK TOO

Yeah, and sombody wrote on your chair, too.

Me going to teach Ook and Glook a lessen once and for all!

Hims name not Glook, it "Gluk". it ryme with "Duck."

Me no care what hims name ryme with! Lets just go arest them!!!

ZONG

So off they went.

it also ryme with "Stuck!"

and "Truck"

One hour Later, They arived at OOKS and GLUKSES caves.

oh, and "Buck"

Dont for-ger "Luck"

SCHAD-OWSKI

JONES

ALRight You dumb kids your under arest!!!

When Ooks sister, Gak, heard The Comosh-en, she pleeded with chief Goppernopper.

aw have mercy and stuff!

Ooh, Hubba Hubba! Me Think mes in Love!

Ew Gross.

will you mary me?

No way ya dumb head

17

Dont worry GAK, we think of something.

Ook and GLuk thought all day Long...

and all night Long, too.

By the next morning they still hadent thought of anything.

LeTs go for walk. maybe it clear our heads.

OK

So they walked out into the deep Jungle.

maybe we Put red ants in hims Loincloth?

No, that not work.

18

Mog-mog not bad. She just want to proteckt baby.

Ook and Gluk sad now.

me too.

Hey lets save Mog-mog.

OK

catch!

PUUULLL!!!

SNAP!

25

What we do now?

Gluk have idea.

You wait here, Baby Mog-Mog. We be rite back.

Where we going?

To Gorila caves.

DANGER Quick Sand →

?

SOON

Gorila caves

Theres ONE! Lets give him the works!!

Hey! Ya smelly crud face!

Hey, Ya diaper breath!

Hey, ya stinky fish feet!

Me think we made new Freinds!

me too.

Hey, MayBe new Freinds can help sister, Gak!

Yeah!

Lets GO!

Mean-while Back in Cave-Land, a wedding is hap-enning

Do you, chief Gooberpicker, take this--

Thats Gop-pernopper!!

Oh yeah. Do you take Gak to be cave wife?

me DO!

and do you, Gak, take cheif uh... um...

Do you take this Little guy over here to Be Cave husbend?

No way Hozãy!

# FLIP-O-RAMA

## Here's How it Works!!!

### STEP 1
Plase your Left hand inside the dotted Lines marked "Left Hand Here." Hold the Book open FLAT.

### Step 2
Grasp the Right-hand Page with your Right Thumb and index finger (inside the dotted Lines marked "Right Thumb Here").

### STEP 3
Now Quickly Flip the Right-hand Page back and Fourth Until the Pitcher apears to Be Animated!

(For extra Fun, try adding your own Sound afecks.)

# FLiP·O·RAMA # 1

## (Pages 37 and 39)

Remember, flip Only page 37.
While you are fliping, be shure
you can See the Pitcher On
Page 37 And the one on
Page 39.

 IF you Flip QuickLy,
the two pitchers WiLL
Start to LooK LiKe
ONE animated pitcher.

Dont ForgeT to
add your own
Sound Afecks.

Left Hand
Here

Do the Bite Thing

37

Do the Bite Thing

# CHAPTER 2

42

Who you Be?

I'm J.P. Goppernopper!

I'm The C.E.O. of Goppernopper Enterprises, The worlds most evil corporashon.

my name Goppernopper too! maybe we be related?

Of corse! You must be my ainshent caveman ansester!

What all this crazy stuff? Me never see anything like it Before!

Follow me and I'll Show you!

44

...You will end up in the year 2222 AD. This is where Im from. Welcome to the Headquarters of Goppernopper Enterprises.

Here, have a complamentery coffey mug and mousepad.

awesome.

But me no understand how come you need Time Portal?

46

Well, by the year 2222, ALL of earths natural resourses have been used up.

Theres no more trees or oil, and the water is all poluted and stuff.

2222 AD

ZAP

G

Fresh Logs Coming Thru!

So we use this time portal to steal all the trees and oil and water from the caveman days!

We bring it all back to modern Times and sell it for huge profits! cheers!

Hmmm. What you doing seem Reckless and iresponsiBLe! Me Love it!!!

ZAP
OIL
G CAVEMAN WATER only $9.99
G CAVEMAN WATER only $9.99

You Know, Gramps, I Like the way you think! Howd you Like to Work for me?

OK

Great! Your Hired! we wont rest until we have stolen all The trees, OiL, and water from the Past!

How you like some slaves, too?

Slaves?

Yeah. Me know where whole villege of cavemen Live.

Awesome! HAW! HAW! Haw!

48

FLIP-O
RAMA 2

Left hand
Here

Bunches-o-Punches!

RIGHT
THUMB
Here

Bunches-o-Punches!

56

The citizins of Caveland marched for days until They finally came to The Time Portal.

OK, Slaves! Grab a shovel and start diggin!!!

man, me hate being slave.

me too.

Hey!!!

These are 2 Troublemakers me telled you about. Me think they be perfect for Torcher exparíments!

Hmmm. This sounds like fun!

57

58

welcome to Gopper-
nopper Tower --- my
world headquarders
and torcher center.™

60

**STOP THEM!**

meanwile...

EXiT

soon our heros found themselfes running for their lifes in a strange futuristic city from the future.

Here they come!

Stop or me shoot!

me too!

Quick hide behind this sign.

our

65

scratch
scratch

They went that-a-way!

You may hide in my school if you like.

Gee Thanks.

trash

MASTER WONG'S School of KUNG-FU

67

That night, Master Wong's daughter, Lan, cooked a big dinner. Ook and Gluk told them everything that happend.

What we do now?

Hmmm...

You must stay ~~over~~ here and Learn the ways of Kung-Fu.

Then when you are ready, Perhapse you can help your family and freinds.

But how? Goppernopper company so big. we just small kids.

There is no Big. no small.

huh?

Look at baby dinosaur. Is she big or small?

That easy. She small.

Lets ask The same Queshtion To this Ladybug.

Yo Man, she Big!

Big and small are oposites. How can both be true at the same Time?

Big and small have no real meaning. Only in your mind.

Therefore you must Look Beyond the surfise to see what is real. In yourselfs and in others.

Boy, Philosofy make my brain hurt.

Yep. That'll happen.

# Chapter 3

Training Time

The next Day

Hey whats your pet dinosaurs name anyway?

Ummm... She no really have name, me guess.

Well Im going To call her Lily cuz Lilies are my faverite flowers.

OK

Today we begin your instruckshon. What is it you wish to Learn?

Me want to learn how to kick butt.

me too.

Those who kick butt are weak. For violens has no mind.

aw man!

If you truley want to set things right, you must walk the Path of Peace.

Here are two white belts. they are simbels of your dedicashen to your training

cool.

When can we learn to use spears and Knifes and stuff?

Those who Truely desire peace must not carry weapons.

For the simple Knife that cuts Bread also cuts flesh.

The Lowley axe That chops wood also chops bones.

chop!

and the commen spear that Kills fish also Kills man.

74

The Best fighters do not show off thier anger.

The wisest warrior wins without a battle.

The flexeble willow Tree does not fight against the storm --- yet it survives.

clay may be shaped into a bowl...

and a house may be formed from Logs...

But it is the spaces within which make these things usefull.

So we must Listen for the spaces within us.

SPLISH

Ook and Gluk studied math, sciense, grammer, speling and chemistry.

They also studied important Things, too.

music and art are like eating and breathing.

One cannot trulely live without them.

Even when Ook and Gluk wern't studying, they were still Learning.

Your minds are free to follow theyr'e own paths. They may soar to the heavens or rot in a prisen. Its up to you!

He who conquers his own mind is the greatest warrier.

The mind is stronger than the flesh. It can defeat any oponent, no matter how strong.

GOPPER-NOPPER TOWER

Ook and Gluk practiced thier Kung-Fu every day.

Soon they got really good.

FLiP-O-RAMA 3

Left hand Here

kung-Fu fever

Right
Thumb
Here

Kung-Fu Fever

Even Lily tried to learn the ways of Kung Fu --- but every time she spinned around, she threw up.

FLIP·O·RAMA 4

Left hand Here

Lily Loses Lunch!

RIGHT
THUMB
here

LiLy Loses Lunch!

Many months passed, and finelly Ook and Gluk had trained for one year.

master wong, when we going to get new belts?

yeah. white belts not too cool anymore.

Master Wong thought for a long time then he asked Ook and Gluk a Queshtion.

Who is the greatest man?

ummmm..

You?

no! No new belts for you.

aw, man!

Another whole year came and went.
Again Ook and Gluk asked about the belts.

We want cool Black Belts!

What we have to do to get Black Belts?

Master Wong asked them the same Queshtion again.

Who is the greatest man?

Ummm

hmmm...

a King?

The President?

No! No black belts for you.

Rats!

One year later, the same thing hapened.

Come on, Please?

Even purple belts be kind of cool.

seeds

Peas

again Master Wong asked the boys:

Who is The greatest man?

me?

me too?

No. No purple belts for you.

Bummer.

92

Years came and went, and Ook and Gluk grew bigger and stronger all the time.

even Ooks missing tooth grew back in.

Me Look awesome!

in your dreams!

But in all that time, they never fig-yured out who the greatest man was.

our ansesters?

no.

The Pope?

no.

Teachers?

no.

a artist?

no.

敬

Popeye?

no.

a woman?

no.

Lily didn't get much bigger, and she never Learned to spin around without barfing, either.

Dad, get the mop!

# CHAPTER 4

## The Heros Jerney

Seven years had come and gone. In that time, Ook and Gluk had grown into men.

the time now come for us to fase us's destiny.

O.K.

Lets go.

oh Ook, Be carefull!!! Dont get hurt!!! I couldent Bear it if any thing bad happened to you!!

Hey what about us?

oh yeah. You too.

Thank you Master Wong. We will do our best to save villege and defeet evil Goppernoppers.

may you have suckse-ss on your Jerney.

Oh, by way, we finelly think we figured out who greatest man is.

and who might that be?

MAST
Sc
Ku

nobody.

MASTER
Scho
Ku

97

Yes. That is corect.

Titles and trophies have no value to the man who is at peace with himself.

True greatness is anonamus. Therefore the greatest man is nobody.

umm... OK...

Well... me guess we better be—

Hey, you dropped something.

WOAH!!! Black Belts!

98

Ook, Gluk, and Lily walked threw the Poluted city toward Goppernopper Enterprises.

these new Black Belts really cool... but me still a little woried.

Remember what master Wong say: "Dont ...umm... Dont be scared and stuff."

But they got Lazer guns and Torcher machines

Master Wong say: "Brains is more awesome than other... umm... stuff. Brains can defeet even strongest enemy guys."

master Wong talk better than you.

Yeah me know. Him have way with words.

Halt! who goes there?

We come in Peace!

Oh yeah? well me gonna Blow You to PEACES !!!

Ooh. Thats a good Line!

Thanks! Me always wanted To Say it but never got chanse until

Hey! where they go?

Left hand
Here

Ook's Rebuke!

RIGHT
THUMB
HERE

Ook's Rebuke!

Left Hand Here

GLUK AMUCK!

Right
thumB
Here

GLUK Amuck!

SOON

We gotta get inside that bild-ing!!!

O.K.

CRASH!

G

Hey, your not alowed to do that!

I'm telling!

Ook, Gluk and Lily searched the strange hallways of Goppernopper Enterprises looking for the Time Portal..........

Polushen departmint

Torcher Room

Stealing Departmint

meanwhile in the security room of That very bilding...

Hey iTs those two Cave Kids who exscaped from our evil clutches seven years ago!!!

security Moniter 7

well they wont exscape again!!!

RELEASE the KiLLeR RoBoTs!!!

SMASH

BOOM BOOM BOOM Boom

The Killer Robots capchered our heros in thier crushing claws.

and only one thing stood in thier way.

LiLy Run!

SAVE yourself!

116

Left hand
Here

Regergitation
Animation

Right
thumb
here.

Regergitation
Animation

So Ook, Gluk, and Lily ran back through the time portal, unaware of the terror that awaited them.

# CHAPTER 5

THE TERROR OF THE

MECHASAURS

When Ook, Gluk and Lily got back to prehistoric times, they dident even reckegnise the place.

Are you shure we in right time?

Yeah. Look at year on time portal.

The three friends searched the raveged land for thier fellow Cavelanders.

Man, saving friends going to be harder than me thinked.

Lets get out of here!!!

atenshon all slaves!!

YOUR GARds have been Kung-fued!!

126

128

me get computer savy in past seven years.

So me uploaded pictures of you into memory banks of mech-asaurs!

me programed them to attack whenever they see your faces! HAW! HAW! Haw!

Sik 'em!

129

The mechasaurs chased OOK, GLUK, and Lily across the horizen...

... and followed them back to 2229 A.D.

Our three heros ran between the many warehouses and stockrooms.

ELECTRIC
SUPLIES

OFFISE
SUPLIES

Finelly they found a good place to hide.

Quick! in Here!

STORAGE ROOM

O.k!

zip

131

134

The mechasaurs crushed each bilding almost as fast as our heros could paint.

But there was STILL one Big bilding That needed To be **CRUSHED**

Gopper-Nopper Tower

Gopper-Nopper Tower

FLIP·O· RAMA **8**

Left hand here

mechasaurus
WRECKS!

RIGHT
THUMB
HERE

mechasaurus
WRECKS!

With Goppernopper Enterprises in Flames and the mechasaurs destroyed, Ook and Gluk vowed to Re-Bild their world.

They started by sending chief Goppernopper and his evil workers back to the year 2229 AD.

aw, man!

ZAP

now it time to find your mom!!!

But before they got a chanse, a paper airplane sailed through the time portal.

Gluk unfolded the paper and read the horrible message.

atenchen Ook and Gluk,
I have capchered master Wong and his doughter. Give up now or they will be killed to death!
Sincerely yours,
J.P. Goppernopper

Ook, Gluk and Lily Returned To the future to save thier friends.

2229 AD

ZAP

Well well well Look whose is here!!!

Did you guys think you could just destroy my empire and get away with it?

Yeah.

Kind of.

WELL YOU CANT!

You destroyed what I Love, so Im going to destroy what you Love!!!

146

148

# HAW! HAW! HAW!!!

HOW we ever going To get out of this?

remember your training my child.

Ook and Gluk closed thier eyes and tried to remember all the wise stuff that Master Wong had told them.

The mind is stronger than the flesh. It can defeat any oponent, no matter how strong.

Gopper-nopper tower

The wizest warrior wins without a battle.

True greatness is anonamuss. Therefore the greatest man is...

Finelly, Ook and Gluk got a idea....

150

So are you losers ready to die???

OK. We just have one Queshtion.

What is it?

Who is the Greatest man?

Well, obviousley I'm the greatest man!

Well, it obvious me is greatest man!

Your the Father of my Butt!!!

One day when me have Kids, me going to teach them some MANNERS!!!!!

You? Have Kids? HAH!!! Whose going to mary you? You Look Like a Little salt shaker!

Maybe me teach You Some manners!

You couldent teach a skunk to stink, You dumb old caveman!!!

at Least me not wear wig!

Left hand
Here

The Pain Event!

RIGHT
THUMB
Here

The Pain Event!

159

If you no longer exist, then neether does your company.

everything you built or created is begining to disapear.

including our ropes and chains.

The world we once knew is being replased by a world without Goppernoppers.

Sudenly Ook and Gluk remembered something important.

The Time PORTAL!!!

Our three Heros ran back to the time portal, which was also starting to disapear.

Quick! It almost Gone!!! Bye master Wong!!!

Bye Lan!

Bye

ZAP

161

master wong Turned and walked back home.

iT was a Jerney he had walked many Times...

...buT This Time was more like a dream.

# EPILOG

502,223 years and 49 minutes earlier...

as the time portal slowly disapeared, the world began to change back to normel.

So OOK, GLUK, Lan and Lily started off on thier Long WALK to Caveland.

and before too Long, they ran into a old friend.

Learn to Speak caveman Language!!!

# CAVEMONICS

**It Fun!**   **It easy!**   **it Annoy Grown-ups!**

| Lesson #1 | Turn "I" into "Me" |
|---|---|

Want to talk Like Caveman? First Rule: No more use Pronoun "I". Instead use "Me"!

## Lets Practise!

| ENGLISH | CAVEMONICS |
|---|---|
| I Like candy. | = Me Like candy. |
| I play baseball. | = Me play baseball! |
| I am awesome. | = Me awesome. |

# LeSSon #2 — SimpLify

Drop any unnese-ssary informashon. ALso, try to find simple replacements for words with more than Two SyLables.

## Lets Practise

| ENGLiSH | | CAVEMONiCS |
|---|---|---|
| I dont care for anchovies on my Pizza. | = | Me no Like little fishes. |
| I'm going to the Local Amusement Park Today. | = | Me go to Barf ride Place. |
| I'd Like to eat at Applebees. | = | me go to Barf place. |

172

# LeSSon #3 — Avoid contractions

Stay away from words like "dont," "cant" and "havent."
Instead try to use the simplest form of the word as a replacement.
In many cases, "no" will do just fine.

## Lets Practise

| ENGLiSH | CAVEMONiCS |
| --- | --- |
| I can't spel very weLL. | = me no speL good. |
| I haven't done my homework. | = me do homework. Dog eat it. |
| my Grandmother doesn't think this book belongs in The School Library. | = Grandma no fun. |

# Lesson #4

Try say everything in "Present tense" whenever you can!

## Lets Practise

| ENGLISH | CAVEMONICS |
|---------|------------|
| I was born on August 14$^{th}$. | = me born one day. |
| Yesterday I went swimming at The water park. | = me catch parasite infection day before now. |
| my annoying next-door-naybors are going to move away This weekend. | = So Long, Suckas! |

See more tips at **WWW.PILKEY.COM**